# Market Treasure Hunt

by Gail Blasser Riley
illustrated by Larry Johnson

MODERN CURRICULUM PRESS
Pearson Learning Group

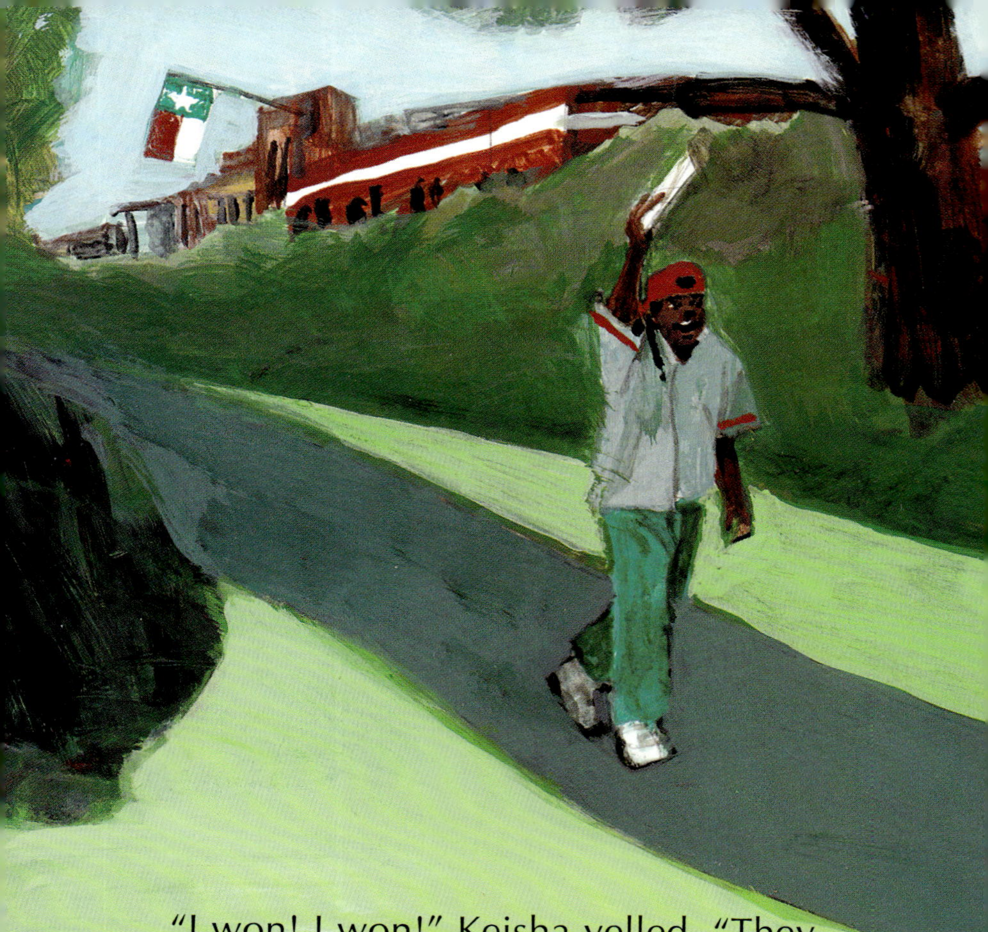

"I won! I won!" Keisha yelled. "They picked my name! I could win tickets to Fun World! I love that place."

"For real?" asked Lena, delighted with her friend's good luck.

"For real," Keisha said. "You and I get to be treasure hunters at the *mercado*—the market in town."

"Not me!" Lena said. "I never win contests. I get so nervous that my brain won't work."

"But you're brilliant, and you're my best friend," said Keisha. "Please?"

"I can't believe I let you talk me into doing this," Lena whispered.

"Here are the rules," said Señor Ruíz. "You have eight minutes to find the clues and get back to the front of the store. Ready? Then get set, GO!"

The girls read the first clue.

Keisha grabbed Lena's hand. "Slow going, slow going, feast. What do you think?"

Lena gulped and opened her mouth, but nothing came out.

"You need a spoon," said Keisha. "I know! Soup! Slow going? Slow soup?" She looked around.

"Turtle soup!" Keisha flipped a can over.

The sun is brilliant.
You're all tapped out.
You do need me
in a drought.

"A camel?" Lena squeaked. "Camel soup?"

"I don't think so," Keisha said. "Quick, only four minutes left. What do you need in a drought? A shower, rain? Water!"

Keisha slipped as she rounded the corner. "Go, Lena! The water! Check the water bottles."

Lena's hands shook so much that water bottles fell all over the floor.

Keisha held up a bottle. "I found it, the last clue."

Keisha shook her head. "This doesn't make sense. Toes? Ground? Help, Lena, help!"

Lena gulped and took a deep breath.

"Speedy," she said. "That must be important. I know—fast! Say it fast. Let us and toe may toes. LETTUCE and toe may toes. LETTUCE AND TOMATOES! Come on!"

"Add something ground. GROUND BEEF! Lettuce, tomatoes, ground beef . . . tortillas? Burritos!" said Lena.

"Fifty seconds," Señor Ruíz shouted.

"Where are the burritos?" Keisha cried.

"Ten seconds," said Señor Ruíz. "Nine, eight, seven . . ."

"Here they are!" Lena yelled as she grabbed the box.

"Two, one!" said Señor Ruíz. "I am delighted to say we have winners!"

Lena looked at the tickets.

"You take them," she said to Keisha. "You got most of the clues. Besides, Fun World is your favorite place in the whole world."

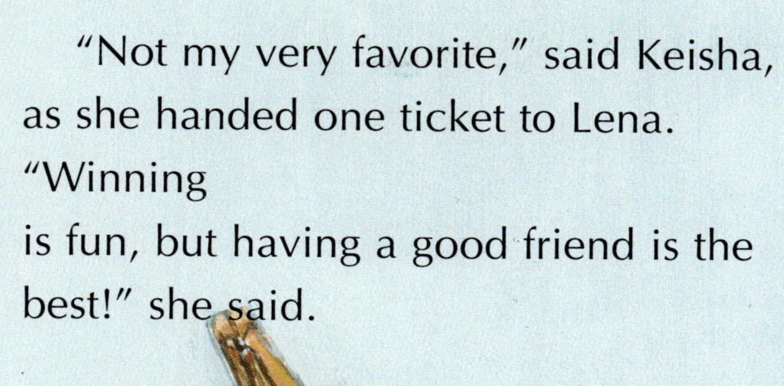

"Not my very favorite," said Keisha, as she handed one ticket to Lena. "Winning is fun, but having a good friend is the best!" she said.